SOCCER MAD

SOCCER MAD
A CORGI YEARLING BOOK : 0 440 86344 9

First publication in Great Britain

PRINTING HISTORY
Corgi Yearling edition published 1996

Copyright © 1996 by Rob Childs
Illustrations copyright © 1996 by Aidan Potts
Cover illustration by Derek Brazell

Set in 12/15pt Linotype Century Schoolbook by
Phoenix Typesetting, Ilkley, West Yorkshire

Corgi Yearling Books are published by Transworld Publishers Ltd,
61–63 Uxbridge Road, Ealing, London W5 5SA,
in Australia by Transworld Publishers (Australia) Pty Ltd,
15–25 Helles Avenue, Moorebank, NSW 2170
and in New Zealand by Transworld Publishers (NZ) Ltd,
3 William Pickering Drive, Albany, Auckland.

Printed and bound in Great Britain by
Cox & Wyman Ltd, Reading, Berkshire.

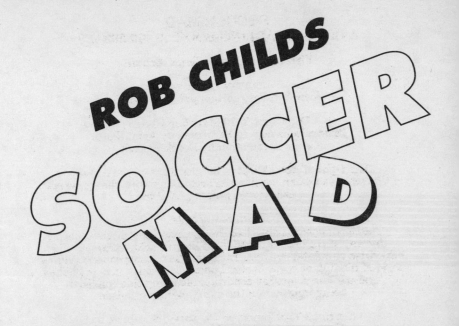

ROB CHILDS
SOCCER MAD

ILLUSTRATED BY
AIDAN POTTS

YEARLING BOOKS

For all soccer mad readers – and players!

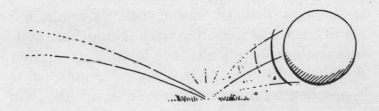

1 Unlucky Thirteen

'Pass it, Luke, pass it!' screamed the school team's captain.

Matthew was wasting his breath. No way was Luke Crawford going to pass the ball. He'd hardly had a kick yet, so he meant to keep it to himself for as long as possible. Sadly, as usual, that wasn't very long. He lost it the moment an opponent bothered to step in and take it off him.

'You loony!' Matthew cried. 'You're just running round in circles like a headless chicken!'

'Cool it, Matt,' Jon told him. 'He's doing his best.'

'Huh!' grunted the captain. 'If this is his best, I just hope he's not in my team on a bad day.'

Jon smiled and gave a little shrug of the shoulders. 'Don't blame Luke. We weren't exactly winning when he came on.'

Matthew snarled. He needed no reminding about the thrashing they were taking. 'Admit it, he's useless. You don't have to stick up for him all the time, you know, just 'cos he's your cousin.'

Jon had no chance to respond to the jibe. The rasping voice of the referee, their sports teacher, 'Frosty' Winter, cut across them. 'Break up the coffee morning chat, you two, and get on with the game. No wonder you're losing eight–nil.'

Stung into action, Matthew moved off moodily in search of the ball once more. He caught up with it at the same time as Luke.

'Foul!' Luke protested as Matthew barged him out of the way.

Frosty showed him no sympathy. 'You can't be fouled by one of your own men. And I bet he's going to score now, you watch.'

Luke watched. Matthew weaved skilfully past two defenders and then steered a low shot beyond the keeper's dive into the corner of the net. The scorer slipped Luke a sly smirk as he jogged by for the re-start. 'See that, eh? That's

why *I* need to have the ball, Loony Luke, not you.'

Luke pulled a face, but left it at that. It didn't pay to answer Matthew back. For one thing, the captain was as good with his fists as with his feet. And for another, Luke desperately wanted to play more games for Swillsby Comprehensive's Year 8 soccer team.

This was a rare chance for Luke to wear the school's black and white stripes. Their soccer squad had been hit by a flu bug and only twelve boys had turned up at the last practice. Luke was one of them, of course. He was always there. He never missed a session, but the only Crawford name to appear on each team sheet was followed by the initial J for cousin Jon.

'Looks like we'll be scraping the bottom of the barrel to raise a team this week,' Frosty had remarked sourly. 'Anybody still standing up on Saturday morning will probably get a game.'

Luke didn't like how Frosty had looked his way as he mentioned 'barrel scraping', but he was too excited to care. He knew he could stand up as well as anybody – it was just the moving about bit with a ball at his feet that he wasn't so good at.

Luke had been the first to report to the school changing rooms that morning, counting the others in one by one. He stuck at ten, and it was only after the convoy of cars from Grimthorpe had discharged their cargo of noisy young footballers that two more latecomers arrived.

'Sorry we're late, sir,' one of them apologized. 'My kid brother's been sick overnight.'

Frosty groaned and peered at the identical Garner twins, stalling for time as he tried to work out which one had the paler face. 'Er, right . . . so, er . . . Gary, how are you feeling now?'

'He's Gregg, sir,' grinned the healthier-looking one. 'I'm Gary, and I'm fine, thanks!'

'Er . . . yes, sorry, Gary,' Frosty stumbled, before turning his attention back to the other. 'Right then, Gregg, so are you OK to play or not?'

Luke listened in, holding his breath for Gregg's answer. 'Mum says I can give it a try, but I must come off if I'm feeling bad.'

Two hearts sank. Luke's because he wasn't needed now in the starting eleven, and Frosty's because his one and only sub would no doubt have to be used sooner or later. Hopefully later. Judged on past experience, the teacher tended to regard Luke as something of a jinx on his team's

13

fortunes. He chucked a shirt Luke's way.

'Number thirteen. Seems the most appropriate number for you,' he said gruffly. 'Sorry, can't find the twelve shirt anywhere.'

Luke wasn't bothered. He wasn't superstitious. Nothing mattered more than the fact that he was included again at last, and he was optimistic about his chances of actually coming on. At least that would be an improvement on his one previous sub's role this season when the only time he got on the pitch was during the pre-match kickabout.

He wondered whether old Frosty still bore a grudge against him for what happened that day. Purely by accident, he'd sliced one of the footballs towards the teacher, hitting Frosty right between the legs with a sickening thud. Served him right, Luke felt, for not watching what was going on. Frosty didn't speak to him for a week. In fact, come to think of it, Luke couldn't remember him speaking to anybody for quite some while afterwards.

The omens had not been good right from the first kick-off. The Reds of Grimthorpe broke clean through the middle and scored before a Swillsby player had even touched the ball. And they followed it up with a series of swift-passing, pacy attacks that stretched the home defence to the limit.

Shots rained in on Sanjay in goal and it was clear to everyone that the two sides were hopelessly mismatched. Maybe at full strength, Swillsby might have been able to give Grimthorpe a more competitive game, but today it was no contest.

Sanjay was the only person who seemed to be enjoying himself. The tall, gangly, Asian keeper

loved being kept busy, throwing himself all around his penalty area to keep the attackers at bay. Mixed in among some good brave stops, however, were his usual collection of gaffes and howlers. Prone to fumbling the ball at heart-stopping moments, he also let one shot slip through his legs and dived right over the top of another bobbling, goal-bound effort.

The fact that the half-time scoreline was only 5–0 was thanks partly to luck, the woodwork being Sanjay's most valuable ally, and partly to Frosty disallowing two more goals for offside.

'We've got the wind behind us second half,' Luke piped up as the mud-spattered team huddled together in a forlorn group. 'Boot the ball upfield to Jon and we can still cause them some problems. Their goalie looks a bit suspect to me.'

'What d'yer mean, *suspect*? He hasn't even had to move yet!' Matthew mocked him. 'He's been leaning on the post most of the time.'

'Exactly!' Luke enthused. 'Over-confidence, that's his trouble.'

'OK, OK,' Frosty said to get their attention. 'I'll decide on tactics, thank you, Luke. We'll need more like a tornado this half to ruffle that

goalie's feathers, not just a bit of breeze.'

The teacher checked on his number ten. 'What about you, er, Gregg?' Even with numbers on their backs, Frosty didn't use the twins' names with any confidence. If Gregg had swapped shirts with Gary, Frosty wouldn't have been able to tell the difference. The boy, though, didn't need to reply. He had spent most of the first half standing alone in the centre-circle, waiting in vain for any passes out of defence. Not that he was well enough to have chased anything that might have come his way.

'Right, I guess we'll have to bring on our secret weapon of destruction,' Frosty announced, reluctantly giving Luke the nod. 'Take over in attack from Gregg and let's see you use this wonderful wind-power of yours.'

The players trooped back into position, bracing themselves for the continued pounding they were sure to undergo. Jon slapped his cousin on the back. 'You've deserved this chance, Luke. Show old Frosty what you can do this half.'

'If the ball ever comes anywhere near me,' Luke grinned.

'If it doesn't, go looking for it yourself. Get in the game.'

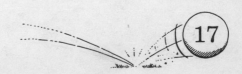

Luke was determined to do just that. *He* wasn't going to stand still, getting cold. Wherever the ball went, Luke attempted to follow it, scampering around all over the pitch. Matthew bellowed to him to hold his position up front but it was no use.

Now that Luke had sampled a taste of the action, his enthusiasm got the better of him. He just couldn't help himself. He became a nuisance to friend and foe alike, not just by getting in the way and falling over the ball, but even more so by his irritating habit of conducting a running commentary on the game, according to how only *he* saw it.

'And here's supersub, Luke Crawford, once
more in the thick of things – Ow! – as he painfully
blocks that ferocious shot at goal and then
cleverly dribbles the ball out of his own penalty
area. Oh! – he's been robbed by a wild tackle
that's gone totally unpunished by the referee . . .'

Still the score mounted up. Matthew didn't
even trust Luke to kick off each time, re-starting
the match himself with Jon. But the ball was
soon lost again and Swillsby had to work hard to
win it back.

Their cause was made even more hopeless
when another player had to go off, heavy-legged
with the lingering effects of the flu. With no

reserves, Swillsby had to play on, a man short, and Grimthorpe finally reached double figures. The tenth goal was perhaps the best of the game.

'*A neat move down the right wing results in a hard, low cross into the six-yard box, met with a text-book flying header . . .*'

Sanjay had no chance. His desperate, acrobatic dive was to no avail, the ball brushing his outstretched hand before smacking into the netting. It was a classic goal, a real stunner, but there were no celebrations from the scorer's teammates.

Sheepishly, the number thirteen picked himself up from the ground, unable to meet anybody's eye. 'Sorry, guys,' Luke mumbled. 'Just trying to head the ball out of danger.'

'You sure did that,' Sanjay sighed as some of the Reds cruelly ruffled Luke's mop of fair hair to rub his embarrassment in further. 'There's no safer place than the back of the net. Nobody can get at it there.'

'Typical!' Frosty muttered under his breath. 'The headless chicken's gone and shown he's got one after all!'

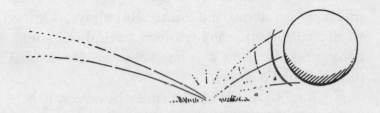

2 What's the Score?

Luke's magnificent own goal was the talk of Year 8 on the Monday morning. Many found it almost impossible to believe that someone so lacking in skill could have scored such a goal.

'Pity it was at the wrong end,' laughed a class-mate at break.

'Doesn't matter,' added another. 'They all count, don't they, Luke? I bet you've already added it to your personal goal tally for the season. How many have you got now, I wonder?'

'Minus one!' quipped Matthew as he came into the room to collect a soccer magazine from his locker.

It wasn't just Luke's antics on the pitch that the others found funny. He was also teased for being a walking, talking encyclopedia of football trivia, a veritable bottomless pit of useless information about the game. But they all knew where to come if they wanted to find out something and Matthew was no exception. He needed to pick Luke's brain.

He had to wait his chance, however, while Luke protested his innocence. 'Look, my goal didn't make any difference to the result,' he said hotly. 'Old Frosty's got no idea how to run a football team.'

To his surprise, Matthew agreed with him. 'Eleven–one, it finished up,' the captain said in disgust. 'Reckon I might even pack up school matches and just play for the Panthers on Sundays in future.'

'How did you get on yesterday?' Luke asked, glad to change the subject.

'Won of course. Beat our nearest challengers to put us five points clear at the top of the league.'

'Did Jon score?'

'Yeah, he got a couple. And how many did your Sloths get stuffed by this time?'

'The *Swifts*,' Luke corrected him.

Matthew failed to stifle a laugh when he heard the score. 'Fifteen–nil! That's even worse than the school team.'

'So?' Luke retorted. 'This is our first season and at least we're getting better.'

'Yeah, it was eighteen last week!' Matthew chortled. 'Sanjay will be getting a bad back with all that bending to pick the ball out the net. Twenty-six goals he let in this weekend. Must be some kind of record, even for him. But then, you should know all about that, Loony Luke . . .' Matthew bit his lip. He wished he hadn't just used that particular nickname. 'Er, anyway, Luke, my old mate,' he continued, trying to sound friendly and holding up his copy of *Great Game!* 'There's a footie quiz in this mag here . . .'

'Oh, yeah,' Luke replied, affecting indifference.

'And they're offering wicked prizes, right. Soccer books, footballs, tracksuits, the lot, plus a complete team strip for the main winner.'

Luke's interest quickened. His Sunday team, the Swillsby Swifts, could certainly do with a proper kit. They were having to turn out in a rag-bag collection of various shades of orange and yellow shirts, off-white shorts and whatever

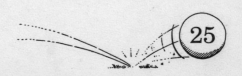

coloured socks each player could find at the last
minute among the dirty washing.

'Go on, then, try me,' Luke said, unable to
resist the temptation to show off a little in front
of the other boys.

He reeled off for Matthew the name of a club's
football ground, another team's manager, the
most capped player for Scotland, the brothers
who had won World Cup medals for England –
but then hesitated on the next stiffer question.
'Hmm, tricky one, that,' he replied. 'Might have
to check through my reference material at home
to help you there . . .'

The bell went at that point and Luke slipped away, grinning. He knew the answer all right, but decided to keep it to himself. 'First of January, 1891, the first time nets were used on goalposts,' he murmured. 'The same year that Blackburn Rovers beat Notts County three—one in the F.A. Cup Final, and James Forrest's fifth winner's medal is still a record. Think I might just go in for that competition myself . . .'

Luke was recognized not only as an expert on the professional game, but as the school team's unofficial statistician too. He kept all the facts and figures of their own matches in a little black notebook, neatly logged in his microscopic handwriting. Even Frosty sometimes consulted him if he needed reminding who scored in last month's 5–2 defeat, or who played on the wing against some team the previous season.

Luke's records went right back to his days at the village primary school. The entries were mostly in black ink, but what stood out were those in red. They were reserved for the special occasions when Luke himself was playing, charting his own career in the minutest detail.

Unhappily for Luke, the red ink had all but dried up. After making eight eventful appearances for Swillsby Primary, five as substitute

but scoring two goals, he had only once actually started a game in his first year at the Comprehensive. His debut was not a great success. The team lost a friendly 7–2 against their arch-rivals, Padley High School, with Luke crazily giving away three penalties.

Frosty's lack of encouragement at least had one consolation. And what an important one it was too. Luke had pestered his dad and uncle until they'd agreed to start up a Sunday League team just for local village lads. They even let Luke sign up the ones he wanted to play for them – mostly those who, like him, could not get much of a look-in at school. Every Swillsby Swifts fixture was now recorded in a brand new notebook, complete with a full match report. In red. After all, he *was* their skipper!

Frosty Winter decided to put his Year 8 squad to the test. 'I've fixed up a special challenge match for you against our Year Sevens,' he told them at a practice session. 'Let's see who comes out on top.'

There was a storm of bravado from most of the boys, eager to put the younger lads in their place. They'd had to suffer quite a bit of stick from them since their recent disaster.

'We'll slaughter 'em!' boomed their tall, short-sighted centre-back, known to everyone as Big Ben.

Matthew, however, was not so sure he liked the idea. His pride was at stake. 'They've got some useful players, haven't they, sir?'

'Promising. They've had a few good wins already – which is more than I can say for you lot. Only one win in five matches so far this season.'

'Six,' Luke said, putting the teacher right.

Frosty glared at him. 'Right, six. That makes it even worse.'

'Bet we could thrash them even with Luke in the team,' Gary giggled.

Frosty joined in the laughter. 'Reckon you'd probably need Luke on their side, Gregg!'

'I'm Gary, sir. Gregg's my kid brother.'

'Hey, less of that kid stuff!' Gregg retorted. 'I'm only younger by ten minutes.'

'So that makes you the baby of the family, junior,' Gary smirked.

It was left to Jon to speak up on Luke's behalf. 'Why don't you let us prove it, sir? You know, give Luke another game, and we'll still win.'

Matthew shot Jon a warning glance, but it was too late. A wicked grin was spreading across Frosty's puffy face. 'Hmm, well, OK, why not?' he replied. 'Might make it more interesting. As long

as our *leading scorer* here promises to keep out of his own penalty area!'

Luke was used to Frosty's attempts at sarcasm at his expense. The sports teacher seemed to take delight in picking on certain people and he was one of them. Others might have lost heart when Frosty kept ridiculing their mistakes, but Luke was determined not to be put off. He loved his football, even if things didn't always work out quite how he might wish.

Sometimes, things didn't even start out the way he hoped. Three days later, his Year 8 team found themselves trailing 2–0 inside the first ten minutes of the game.

That was humiliating enough without the memory of his own glaring miss. Jon had unselfishly squared the ball to him after drawing the Year 7 keeper off his line and all Luke had to do was tap the ball into the open goal. But in his excitement, already picturing himself wheeling away towards the touchline, one arm raised in celebration, he committed the fatal error. He took his eye off the ball. As it rolled invitingly into his path, he swung at it hastily and failed to make any contact whatsoever. Luke finished up crumpled in a heap, taunted by the

chorus of jeers and cheers alike.

By half-time, however, Matthew had pulled a goal back and the captain now demanded a huge effort from his side as they changed ends. 'If we lose this match, we'll never hear the last of it,' he warned. 'Show some guts!'

Sanjay, as usual, made a joke of it. 'We'll let Tubs do that for us. Lift your shirt up, Tubs, and frighten them kids with your rolls of fat!'

The substitute full-back grinned, unruffled by the playful insult, and did indeed make his large presence felt. Encouraged by Sanjay to 'Give it some welly!', he put his full weight behind a clearance to hoof the ball right up into the oppo-site penalty area and allow Gregg to scramble the equalizer.

Soon it was time for Luke to use his head once more. Or to be more precise, his face. *'And here's Luke Crawford, back to help out his defence at a corner, guarding the goal-line as the striker shoots . . .'*

He was too slow to duck out of the flight path of the ground-to-net missile and his shrill com-mentary was cut off dead as if the microphone had been snatched from under his squashed nose. Blood streamed down onto his striped shirt

and a dazed Luke was helped off the field to the medical room to be cleaned up. 'I'll be back,' he promised. 'Hold out!'

The Year 8 side did more than just hold out. They won. Luke reappeared on the touchline, hoping in vain to be allowed back on, just in time to see his cousin perform a piece of magic. Jon killed a dropping ball with one silky touch on the turn before gliding past the advancing keeper to stroke them into a 3–2 winning lead.

When Frosty blew the final whistle, Jon trotted over to inspect the damage. 'Don't know what you were doing standing on the line, Luke, but it's a good job for us that you were there. Saved a certain goal.'

Luke managed a sort of lop-sided smile, thinking he might even enter his injury in his notebook in red blood. 'Yeth,' he replied nasally. 'How to be in the wrong plathe at the right time!'

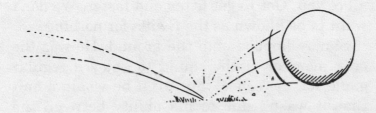

3 Swillsby Swifts

'C'mon, men, run, run, run! Faster, faster!'

Luke was putting the small squad of Swifts' players through their paces in training, urging them on in a series of sprint relays.

'I notice . . .' panted Big Ben, drawing in great gulps of air, 'that you . . . are not doing . . . much running . . . Skipper.'

Luke looked hurt. 'I can't run and coach at the same time, can I?' he reasoned. 'I've got to be able to see what's going on everywhere, see who might be slacking. Your turn again, quick, go, go, go!'

Big Ben lumbered off once more, twisting in and out of the slalom course of cones before heading back towards his team, accompanied by Luke's croaked commands. 'C'mon! Sprint back, all of you. Got to get fitter and faster. We don't want to be known as the Swifts for nothing.'

Sanjay flopped onto the ground. He was the only member of the squad to enjoy a regular game for the school, but even he would admit that it wasn't due to his ability between the posts. There was just nobody else in their year group who wanted to play in goal. 'That's enough, Skipper,' he groaned. 'I'm done in. Goalies don't have to go charging around all over the pitch like other players.'

'Goalies still have to be fit,' Luke argued. 'What if you've got to race outside your area to beat some attacker to the ball? You have to be quick off the mark like a sprinter out of his blocks.'

The relays ground to a halt as all the other players decided to take an unscheduled breather too. 'C'mon, men, up on your feet again,' Luke demanded. 'People are already calling us the Sloths.'

'They can call us what they like,' Tubs

wheezed. 'Some of us are just not built for sprint-
ing, Luke.'

'Skipper.' Luke reminded him of his preferred
title at Swifts' practice sessions. 'I know that,
Tubs, but we're giving away too many goals
through tiredness near the end of games. A good
team needs players with stamina and speed as
well as skills.'

'Sounds like you've been reading too many
coaching books,' Sanjay laughed.

Luke flushed. 'Somebody's got to do the coaching. And seeing as I'm skipper . . .'

'You're only skipper because the Crawford

family run the whole show,' interrupted Sean, their left-footed midfielder.

'Leave off, Sean,' cut in Mark, Big Ben's partner in central defence. 'The Swifts *were* Luke's idea in the first place, remember.'

'Thanks, Mark, but maybe Sean's got a point,' Luke said seriously. 'Anyone think that somebody else should be skipper and not me?'

Luke waited, heart in mouth, for one of them to speak up. But when Big Ben did finally break the embarrassed silence, it amounted to a vote of confidence.

'It's OK, Skipper, none of us really wants the job anyway, so there's no need to get your knickers in a twist,' he said to raise a laugh. 'We don't mind you trying to boss us about a bit so long as you do your fair whack in training as well.'

Luke breathed a sigh of relief. 'Right, so let's get down to work again, men,' he grinned. 'I want us to practise our set-piece moves at corners. That's not too energetic for some of you, I hope, is it?'

They giggled, happy at the chance to start kicking a ball about after all the stretching exercises and running. Luke reminded them of his chalked diagrams, showing their positions

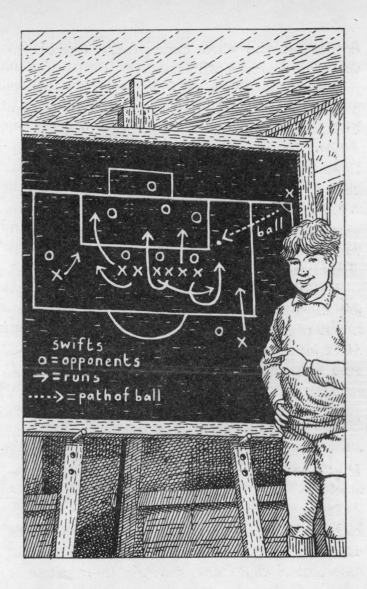

swifts
o = opponents
→ = runs
·····> = path of ball

and the directions in which to make their darting runs to find space. It had been confusing enough on the blackboard. On the pitch, the first time they tried it out, it was a shambles. Most went the wrong way and collided with one another.

Luke picked himself up off the ground. 'Let's just go through that again, shall we, men?' he grunted.

Luke's dad, Philip, was watching from behind the goal. 'A good tactic, this, don't you think, Ray?'

'What?' asked his younger brother, trying to read a newspaper.

'Luke getting Sean to do inswinging corners from the right wing with that educated left foot of his.'

'Educated left foot!' Ray scoffed. 'You're beginning to sound like one of Luke's commentaries. The way Sean keeps hooking the ball towards us standing here, I reckon his left foot must have failed its exams!'

'Aye, well, he's going to need a lot more practice to get it right.'

'He sure is. Do you think we ought to get somebody in to give the lads some proper coaching?'

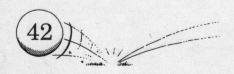

Philip looked up at his taller, bearded brother. 'What do you mean by that? Don't you think that my Luke's doing things right then?'

Ray gave his usual vague shrug, a mannerism copied by his own son, Jon. 'Suppose so, but how can we tell? What us two know about the game wouldn't even half-fill a football. I just thought . . .'

'Well, don't. Luke lives for this game. Being captain of the Swifts is the best thing that's ever happened to him.'

'Fine, but getting hammered every week can't be doing much for the lads' spirits, can it?'

'Luke will get them sorted out, you'll see. Anyway, the boys don't seem to mind, they just love playing. We don't want that "win-at-all-costs" kind of attitude here that some Sunday teams seem to have.'

'Are you having a dig at the Panthers again?' Ray asked accusingly. 'My Jon's under no pressure from me.'

'I know that,' said Philip. 'But what about the way some parents behave on the touchline? Ranting and raving at their kids if they make the slightest mistake – mums as well as dads!'

Ray chuckled and removed his glasses to clean them. 'Well, at least we don't have that sort of bother. Hardly anybody comes to watch the Swifts!'

As Sean swept another corner out of play, his teammates fell about laughing. 'What a wally!' hooted Sanjay. 'Just look at him posing by the corner flag. He's more concerned that he's got his hair in the right place than the ball!'

Luke was losing his patience. 'What's the point of all us attackers shaking off our markers if the ball ends up in the crowd every time?'

44

'Crowd!' echoed Dazza, one of the wingers, his face creased up into a sparkling grin. 'Who are you trying to kid, Skip? This isn't Old Trafford, you know!'

'Well, OK, then,' Luke muttered. 'Ends up in the brook, if you prefer. You want to have a go yourself?'

'No way, man. Last time I tried to take a corner, I kicked the flag out of the ground.'

'What about you, Brain?' Luke asked, turning in desperation to their other winger. 'You've got two good feet on you.'

'Huh!' the boy grunted, slouching over

towards the corner. 'Only 'cos I can't tell which is right from left.'

'Well, try hitting it with your left.'

He looked down at his feet. 'Which one's that?'

'The one next to your right,' Luke answered unhelpfully. 'Just go and take it, will you, or we'll be here all night.'

To their surprise, the ball soared over into the goalmouth bang on target. Such was the shock that nobody made a move for it and it bounced harmlessly through to the far touchline.

'Great stuff, Brain!' Luke yelled. 'Just testing! Now prove it wasn't a fluke by doing it again and this time we'll be ready.'

'Why do they call him Brain?' Ray asked.

'Well, it's Brian really, but he can't always get the spelling of it right,' Philip smiled. 'He's a bit dyslexic or something. You know, not very good with his letters and all that.'

The winger approached the next kick from the same direction, but this time suddenly hit the ball with the outside of his right boot. Luke and the other players, forwards and defenders alike, failed to guess which way the ball was heading and could only gawp as it swerved back over their heads and dropped into the goal without anyone else touching it.

'Amazing!' Ray exclaimed. 'Who cares if you can't spell when you can do things like that with a ball?'

The practice continued until it was almost too dark to see both goals. 'Time to switch on the floodlights, Skipper!' Sanjay joked.

Luke had barely noticed. He was too wrapped up in their seven-a-side game, playing, coaching and refereeing it at the same time. Not to mention thinking furiously about his starting line-up for Sunday's match.

'What's the team, then?' Mark asked as they all gathered up their gear.

'I'll let you all know at school tomorrow,' Luke announced. 'I've got to sleep on it yet. Been thinking of making a few changes.'

They groaned. Luke was always tinkering with the line-up, trying people out in different positions as he came up with new tactical plans which they rarely understood. They doubted whether he really did either.

'Wish you'd stick with the same formation for more than five minutes,' Brain said. 'You get me all muddled. I never know which side of the pitch I'm supposed to be on.'

'That's the beauty of it,' grinned Sanjay. 'If *you*

don't know where you are, the other team have got no chance of marking you!'

Luke ignored them. 'We're playing at home against a team called Carlton Vale. They're near the top of the league so they're bound to be a bit useful. We'll have to be on top form to beat them.'

Tubs let out his familiar rumbling laugh. 'Just listen to him – ever hopeful. We'll have to be on top form merely to keep the score down to single figures.'

'Rubbish! Wait till you see our two big new signings.'

They all looked at Luke in astonishment. 'What two big new signings?' Dazza demanded. 'First I've heard of this.'

'And me!' echoed the others.

'Come on, don't keep us in suspense,' Sanjay urged. 'Who are these superstars? Have you poached Jon and Matt from the Panthers?'

'Nope,' beamed Luke, delighted to have kept the secret to himself for so long. 'I've persuaded the Garner twins to come and play for us.'

'Gary and Gregg!' Sanjay snorted in derision. 'The Gee-Gees! Blimey, things must be bad if we've had to send for the cavalry to rescue us!'

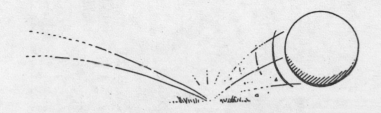

4 Action Replay

'Right, men,' Luke began, tugging at his dark, captain's armband. 'All ready?'

'Ready, Skipper!' they chorused, laughing a little self-consciously at their well-rehearsed ritual before a match.

Luke liked to give his team a pep talk in the changing cabin before they went out on to the village pitch. He looked around at the bizarre collection of kit. Apart from himself of course – the only one with a number on the back of his shirt, a white, three-dimensional figure nine – he felt that only Sanjay really looked the part.

The extrovert keeper was resplendent in a snazzy, multi-coloured goalie top with green shorts, socks and matching gloves.

'OK, we know we're in for a tough match – but so are Vale,' Luke went on, undeterred. 'Don't be put off by their smart, sponsored strip – it's all for show, just like Sanjay's here.'

'Hey, watch it, Skipper,' Sanjay grinned. 'Don't dent my ego!'

Luke ignored his interruption. 'They're just like us underneath . . .'

'What? Useless?' Tubs put in quickly to much hilarity, especially as Luke was still trying to be so serious.

'Let's go out there and show 'em how we can play,' he finished.

'Good idea, Skipper,' said Titch, their pocket-sized ragamuffin in midfield. 'They'll be too busy laughing at us then to play properly themselves.'

Luke clapped his hands to restore some sort of order and urged them to run out as a team on to the field. The effect was rather spoiled, however, when Brain missed his footing on the cabin's small flight of wooden steps and toppled forwards, bringing down several others with him like a riderless horse at a Grand National fence.

The Swifts could never have imagined what a dream start to the match they were going to enjoy after that. In their first attack, Dazza collected a mis-hit pass from Titch and set off down the right wing. He managed to stumble past one challenge but as another defender loomed into view, he panicked and lashed the ball away. It went straight into the goalkeeper's hands but immediately popped out again, dropping at Luke's feet. It was a golden opportunity that even Luke could not miss, toe-poking the loose ball over the line from all of a metre out.

Maybe it was the unexpected, excited voice in his ear that put the goalie off. *'In comes Dazza's curling cross as skipper Luke Crawford lurks like*

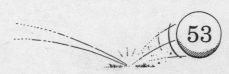

53

a deadly tiger in the six-yard box, ready to pounce on any mistake. And – YES! – the keeper's fluffed it . . . Goooaaalll! . . . Goooaaalll!'

Luke's wild celebrations took him whirling away towards the corner flag, dancing deliriously around it and still screaming his commentary at full volume as if to drown the cheers of fifty thousand ecstatic fans. It was his very first goal for the Swifts, and indeed only their fourth of the whole season so far.

Mercifully, he was eventually muffled under a mob of happy teammates before floating on cloud nine back to the centre-circle, a dreamy, idiotic grin etched across his thin face.

'He's mad!' came a comment from one of the Vale players. 'He's gone totally bananas!'

Luke never heard. He was lost in a fantasy world of his own creation, doing media interviews as part of his continuing, breathless commentary.

His mood gradually calmed down and became more sombre, however, as the goals inevitably began to be clocked up at the other end. *'And there's the fourth, sadly, as Sanjay, the Swifts' brave last line of defence, slips and allows the Vale number eight to sweep the ball into an unguarded net.'*

55

This could be translated less charitably as Sanjay making a complete pig's ear of his attempt to boot a back pass out of play. The keeper missed the ball altogether with his desperate hack and the forward ran on in the clear, unchallenged, to notch up his hat-trick.

Faced with a 5–1 deficit at the interval, Luke pulled his intended master-stroke. He had persuaded Gary to start as sub, ready to take his twin's place up front for the second half. Gregg was exhausted. Told by the skipper to run himself into the ground, he had done his job well. The Vale defence had watched his performance of manic running with awe, convinced he would never be able to keep it up for the entire match.

He didn't have to. Gregg sat out the rest of the game to allow Luke's tactical switch to fool his marker. And it worked! Mid-way through the second period, Sean slid a long through-ball towards the Vale goal for Gary to chase. The defender set off casually, confident that the Swifts' player would have no energy left to win such a race. He could not believe it when the attacker burst past him inside the area and whacked the ball wide of the equally dumbfounded goalie to make the score 8–2.

That was how it stayed until the final whistle, and the sporting defender shook Gary by the hand as they left the field. 'Well done, pal. I'm school cross-country champion but I couldn't keep going like you did.'

'Don't worry about it,' Gary grinned as Gregg approached. 'Er . . . I believe you two guys have already met.'

The defender looked from one twin to the other and blinked. It was like looking at a reflection in the mirror. He shook his head. 'I think I must have taken a knock,' he murmured. 'I'm getting double vision.'

Rain washed out the next Swifts' practice session and Luke jumped at the chance of inviting his players back home to show them a video of the Vale game. It had been shot somewhat haphazardly by Dad from the touchline with the family's new camcorder.

'Where's my ice-cream?' wailed Tubs. 'I always have one when I go to see a film.'

'Just shut up about ice-creams,' Luke snapped, 'and watch how I shoot us into the lead here right at the start.'

The boys collapsed with laughter as they saw

how Luke had danced like a demented demon around the corner flag. 'You seem quite pleased about something, Skipper,' Sanjay remarked drily.

When Dad had handed the tape over to him for editing out all the sequences of grass, trees and sky, Luke duly went about the task with typical zeal. He not only succeeded in erasing Dad's errors but all of his own too, though still retaining in the game's brief highlights any scenes where he somehow managed a decent touch of the ball.

If his dreams of one day playing centre-forward for England were never to come true, he'd discovered that the video camera gave him a wonderful chance to practise his skills for his other ambition in life – that of becoming a tele-vision football commentator. His fanciful, biased version of events, dubbed on to the film, helped to liven up any duller parts of the match for his hysterical audience.

'And now Luke Crawford, the Swifts' skipper, comes over to the touchline, taking responsibility for this important throw-in near the halfway line. The Vale players think he's going to throw the ball in one direction, but suddenly he twists

the other way, selling them a clever dummy, and releases the ball perfectly into Dazza's path . . .'

'How can you sell a dummy just taking a throw-in?' Tubs hooted.

'Easy,' cackled Sanjay. 'You shout out, "Hey! Anybody want to buy a dummy?" before you chuck the ball away from them!'

'What's a *clever* dummy, anyway?' Dazza chipped in, setting himself up for a corny joke. 'One that can speak without moving its lips?'

To their clear disappointment, the film ended

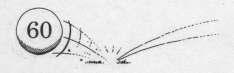

earlier than expected. 'How come we only seemed to lose 3–2?' asked Brain. 'What happened to all the rest of their goals?'

'Hmm, well, it's quite a tricky job, this cutting and editing,' Luke explained. 'Afraid I lost some of the other stuff.'

'Like when you missed a sitter in the second half,' Sean observed.

'Don't remember that,' Luke replied.

'No, you wouldn't,' Big Ben sighed. 'But I noticed you managed to keep my own goal in. It wasn't my fault, I didn't see the ball coming until it was too late.'

'Well, now you've got your specs on, you've been able to spot where you went wrong, haven't you?' said Luke. 'That's the good thing about action replays. You can learn from your mistakes. You obviously shouldn't have been lying on the ground like that in the first place.'

'Got tripped up, didn't I, but your dad never caught that on film of course. Ref didn't see it either. Just my luck!'

'A video nasty, I call that,' said Mark. 'A real horror movie, showing up how bad we really are. I hope you're going to destroy the evidence after this, Skipper.'

'It'll be better once Dad gets more practice with the camera.'

'Yeah, maybe, but will *we* get any better? If this film falls into the wrong hands – like Matt's – it could be dead embarrassing.'

Nobody liked the thought of that. 'OK, OK,' Luke agreed. 'I'll wipe it clean later – apart from my goal of course – and then I can use the tape again to record a school match.'

'Great idea!' cried Sanjay. 'So long as you do a commentary over it as well and then you can sell it at school as a comedy video.'

'Right,' Tubs agreed. 'Or give one copy away free with every clever dummy you sell!'

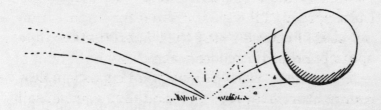

5 Match Reports

Luke's passion for football could not entirely be satisfied by his books of statistics, his computer games, his soccer annuals and coaching manuals, his team posters, pictures and stickers, his new video commentaries or even actually playing. His creative talents needed another outlet – journalism – and this was provided by Uncle Ray who was editor of the *Swillsby Chronicle,* the village's free monthly newspaper. Luke's goal was re-lived in all its glory on the sports page of the next issue.

SWIFTS GO DOWN FIGHTING

by our soccer correspondent

Swillsby Swifts 2 Carlton Vale 8

Despite taking an early lead through a fine, opportunist goal from the trusty right boot of their skipper, Luke Crawford, the Swifts unluckily found themselves trailing by half-time. It was a brave, battling team performance against the high-flying visitors, who benefited from some dubious refereeing decisions. Showing their famous fighting spirit, the Swifts' 'never-say-die' attitude earned them a well-deserved late goal after an inspired substitution by their player-manager. 'Our fitness now matches the best in the league,' said their coach afterwards, reflecting upon the harshness of a narrow defeat. 'We kept going right to the end.'

'Did you read that rubbish about the Sloths in the *Chronicle* the other day?' Matthew scoffed as he got changed for the school team practice. 'A *narrow* 8–2 defeat. What a joke! They got pulverized again.'

'I noticed the scorer of the second goal never got a name-check,' Gary said sourly, knowing that Luke was listening in the corner of the room.

'Don't be daft, Gary, no chance of that,' Matthew continued loudly. 'I mean, by the time the heroic deeds and thoughts of the skipper, player-manager and coach have been recorded, there's little space left for anybody else to get a mention, is there?'

'I wonder who the paper's soccer correspondent can be?' queried Adam, the school's first-choice centre-back, who was also a teammate of Matthew's for Padley Panthers.

'No,' replied Matthew, shaking his head theatrically. 'You've got me stumped there, Adam, my old mate. But whoever it is, he obviously knows nothing about football.'

Luke kept his grim silence, knowing that all eyes were upon him. 'You wait till the next time you come running to me, Matthew, wanting help

with some soccer quiz,' he muttered under his breath. 'Then we'll see who knows about the game all right.'

Frosty appeared at that moment, seemingly in a good mood for a change with a broad grin on his face. 'Sorry I'm late, lads. Just been catching up on my reading.'

He gazed meaningfully over to where Luke was sitting and flourished a copy of the *Chronicle*. 'Best laugh I've had for ages, this. The bit about the skipper's "trusty right boot" really

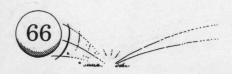

creased me up. They had to scrape me off the staffroom floor . . .'

Luke stood up and went outside to lace his boots, leaving the room in uproar. 'Let them mock, I don't care,' he murmured. 'I won't let them see the video of my scouting trip now. Bet they'd only laugh at that too.'

Luke had been busy. With the next school game being a needle match against Padley High School, he'd persuaded Dad to take him into town so that he could film them in action. At

67

least it was a good excuse to get some practice with the camera himself. A careful study of his match video had shown up a few possible weaknesses in Padley's team, but he decided that Frosty would just have to manage without such valuable insights.

The practice session did not go well for Luke. Nobody called him Skipper here, of course. In fact, hardly anybody spoke to him at all. Or passed the ball to him. Only cousin Jon made any effort to be friendly, consoling him when he wasn't selected to play.

'Another time, eh, Luke? Frosty wants to put out his strongest side to gain revenge for last season's defeat.'

Luke pretended he wasn't bothered. 'Didn't expect to be picked.'

'You'll still come along to watch, though, as always?'

'Might do. I was thinking of bringing the camcorder to record the highlights.'

'Great! We've been taking the mickey out of each other at the Panthers for weeks about this match, bragging how many we're going to score,' Jon grinned. 'It'd be wicked to have a video to show 'em later to rub it in.'

'If you win,' Luke added.

Jon shrugged. 'Well, win or lose, it'd still be a good laugh.'

'Don't you ever take football seriously, Johan?' Luke scowled, using his pet nickname for his cousin after the famous old Dutch footballer, Johan Cruyff. Luke rated Cruyff the best player ever to kick a football.

Jon gave that little casual shrug again, infuriating Luke even more. 'I mean, you just seem to take your skills for granted. You go out on the pitch and perform all your tricks with the ball without even thinking about it. I have to flog my guts out to get any little bit of success I can and everybody still makes fun of me. It's not fair.'

Luke's sudden outburst, releasing all his pent-up frustrations in one long moan, caught Jon unawares. 'Tell you what, Luke, how about the two of us working on some things together secretly in your garden,' he suggested off the top of his head. 'Then you might be able to go out and surprise a few people one day with what you can do. What d'yer say?'

Luke cheered up immediately. 'Yeah, thanks, Johan, brill. And I could perhaps teach *you* how to do flying headers like that one of mine!'

'Here comes number eight, Jon Crawford, Swillsby's Johan Cruyff, swooping on to a pass from Matthew, his captain. Jon feints, drops his left shoulder to throw a defender off-balance while he moves smoothly off to the right with the ball still under perfect control. He looks up, sees that the keeper has strayed off his line and attempts the most delicate of chips from well outside the area. Is it going to drop in? No! The ball flops over the bar and lands on top of the netting. Unlucky!'

Several spectators stared at the raving boy as he skipped along the touchline, juggling a camcorder and yelping out a colourful description of the action. They exchanged glances of amusement and pity. One of them tapped the side of his head and grinned as Luke went by, oblivious of their ridicule. 'Potty!' the man said to the group from Padley. 'I saw him at the High School match the other day. Absolutely bonkers!'

Luke stopped filming for a few moments while he checked his watch and took out his black note-book to record the time of a substitution. *'It looks like Padley are taking a big gamble in their search for that elusive opening goal,'* his commentary droned on. *'They've taken off one of their defenders to bring on another attacker . . .'*

There were still about ten minutes to go. The fact that neither team had been able to break the deadlock was thanks mainly to the exploits of the two goalkeepers.

Much to everyone's amazement, Sanjay had been outstanding, flinging himself about his penalty area and having easily his best ever game for the school. Ravi in the Padley goal was in his usual excellent form, despite being caught out by Jon's clever lob. Luke had heard all about Ravi's brilliance from his cousin and had now seen for himself in the two games he had filmed just how good a keeper he was. But Swillsby were looking increasingly dangerous, enjoying a good spell of pressure on Ravi's goal that finally brought its reward.

Gary linked up well with his twin brother along the left touchline before Gregg suddenly switched play, hitting the ball firmly inside to

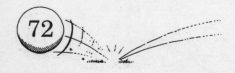

Matthew. The captain's surge forward took him past two defenders and he kept running after slipping the ball to Jon on his right. Jon's first-time return ball was a gem, executing a slick one-two pass with Matthew that gave defenders no chance to intercept.

Without hesitation, Matthew lashed the ball goalwards and, although Ravi got a hand to it, the keeper knew he was beaten. He heard Matthew's shout of triumph an instant before the sound of the ball thwacking into the net behind him.

'With Swillsby Comp now one–nil up, Frosty Winter, the referee and the school's ancient, bad-tempered soccer coach, looks at his watch anxiously as Padley kick off again. Can his team hold out? Is he regretting leaving out one of his key players, Luke Crawford, who surely would have had the match sewn up long before this had he been chosen? Both teams have missed far too many chances . . .'

Tubs, also out of the team, overheard this snatch of the commentary as Luke scurried past him, trying to keep up with another Padley raid. He shook his head and let out a rumbling laugh. 'You live in a dream world, Luke. Get real, will you!'

His remark fell upon deaf ears. Luke was in full flow. 'This is nasty for Swillsby. Adam's nowhere and there are two players unmarked over on the right, screaming for the ball, but the striker looks as though he's going to have a shot himself. Sanjay comes hurtling towards him to narrow the angle and – oh, dear! – just as the number nine tried to sidestep his reckless dive, the keeper has brought him down, crashing into man and ball at the same time. It has to be a penalty, surely! No! The referee is waving play on, ignoring the appeals, and the ball has been

cleared. The player is lying in the area, injured, and the Padley supporters are going berserk . . .'

'Disgraceful!' cried one of the Padley fathers. 'The ref's a cheat. Blatant foul, that.'

He ran up to Luke, interrupting the live commentary. 'Did you get that on film, son?' he demanded. 'That'll prove it was a penalty. We've got video evidence now.'

Luke went red. 'Er, well, actually, no. Sorry!'

'What d'yer mean, no? You must have done.

You've been running up and down the line like a yo-yo all match with that camera.'

'Afraid the battery's gone flat,' Luke said lamely. 'I've just been pretending for the last five minutes.'

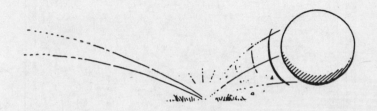

6 The Winner!

'I guess that's one way of missing a penalty!' Jon grinned as Luke told him the sorry tale later that day. 'Forgetting to re-charge your battery!'

'The Padley lot were dead narked,' Luke reflected, shaking his head. 'Frosty ought to be grateful for once that I messed things up again.'

Luke was kitted out in full Swifts' gear and boots for their kickabout on his back lawn, Jon dressed more casually in jeans, T-shirt and trainers. In front of them yawned a small, home-made goal, fixed up by Luke two years before.

Jon couldn't resist the temptation. He flicked a
football up into the air with his left foot and
crashed it on the volley with his right as it
dropped. The ball glanced off the far post and
nestled, still spinning, in the bottom of the tan-
gled netting.

'How did you do that?' Luke gasped. 'You
nearly broke the goal.'

'Don't know exactly. I just do it.'

'See what I mean, Johan. It just comes so
natural to you. I'd be whooping it up around the
garden if I'd done something like that.'

'You'd be writing about it in Dad's *Chronicle*!'
Jon joked.

Luke sighed wistfully. 'What does it feel like
when you actually score the winning goal for a
team?'

'You'd better ask Matt. He scored that one
this morning.'

'Yes, but you've scored the winner loads of times. Describe it.'

Jon shrugged. 'I haven't got a way with words like you, Luke. It's just . . . pure magic! The feeling washes all over you. There's nothing quite like it.'

Luke remembered his excitement after scoring that little tap-in against Carlton Vale and tried to multiply it ten times. It left him all shuddery. 'Show me how I can score more goals, Johan. Go on, what am I doing wrong?'

For the next half an hour, Luke sprayed the goal with shots, some dead ball efforts and some where Jon rolled a pass in front of him to hit on the move. There was no goalkeeper. They didn't need one. Most of the shots went high or wide and disappeared into the shrubbery.

'Take your time,' came Jon's well-meaning advice. 'Don't hurry it. Try not to lean back so much or you'll keep scooping it up in the air.'

Luke, red-faced with exertion, called a temporary halt. 'That's my main problem, I know. I've read about it in all the books, but I can't seem to stop doing it.'

He watched Jon in action, his head still and his body right over the ball as he made contact.

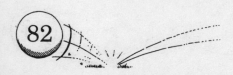

Nine times out of ten the ball zipped low and hard between the posts.

'Wish I could do that,' Luke whistled in admiration.

'Keep practising and you will,' Jon encouraged him. 'And the next thing is to do it in a proper match. Don't panic when you get a shooting chance. You need a cool head.'

Luke's dad appeared in the garden at that moment, brandishing an envelope. 'This came for you earlier,' he explained. 'You'd dashed out the house before the post arrived and then I forgot all about it.'

Luke was puzzled. 'Nobody writes to me,' he said, tearing it open. 'Wonder who it's from?'

'Perhaps it's the England manager calling you up for the squad,' Jon smiled.

Luke slumped down onto the grass in a state of shock, eyes wide, staring at the letter. 'I don't believe it!' he croaked.

'What is it?' asked Dad in some alarm.

Suddenly Luke jumped up, punched the air and then whacked the ball at the goal in sheer exuberance. This was no time for a cool head. The ball cannoned off the underside of the cross-bar to bulge out of the netting.

'*Goooaaalll!*' he shrieked in his wildest commentator's cry. '*The winner! Luke Crawford has won!*'

Jon picked up the letter that his cousin had thrown away in excitement. 'Incredible! Luke's got first prize in that magazine soccer quiz,' he announced. 'He's won a brand new team strip in the colour of his choice!'

'At least we only lost 5–0 last Sunday,' Tubs said, grinning. 'We must be getting better.'

Luke clutched at the straw he was being offered. 'Of course we are, no doubt about it. I reckon we were dead unlucky not to score one or two ourselves. I was sure that shot of mine crossed the line.'

'Yeah, the touchline, Skip!' laughed Dazza.

Luke could afford to smile at playful ribbing like that now. He felt more confident since the competition win and knew that the gold strip he'd chosen for the Swifts was on its way. His name had been printed in bold capitals in the magazine and that had earned him some respect, even envy, at school. Frosty congratulated him, too, but didn't seem so keen once he found out Luke hadn't ordered black and white stripes for the school team.

'C'mon, men, let's get cracking,' he urged as the Swifts changed for training on the Wednesday evening. 'Practice makes perfect, they say.'

'They obviously haven't been to watch us,' Sanjay put in. 'What is it? Played nine, lost nine – and I've lost count of the number of goals we've let in.'

'*You*'ve let in,' Luke corrected his goalkeeper pointedly. 'I haven't lost count, don't worry. And anyway, it's only eight defeats, not nine. One match got abandoned, remember, when Tubs jumped up to swing on the crossbar and snapped it!'

'I was just doing a bit of goal-hanging!' Tub explained, chuckling with the rest at the memory.

'I've been planning out some free-kick routines for us to practise today,' Luke declared, producing a handful of table football figures from his bag to use as models and collecting the blackboard from the corner of the cabin. He ignored the protests and began to draw a mass of lines, circles, crosses and arrows in chalk. 'So before we get out there on the pitch, I want you all to study this . . .'

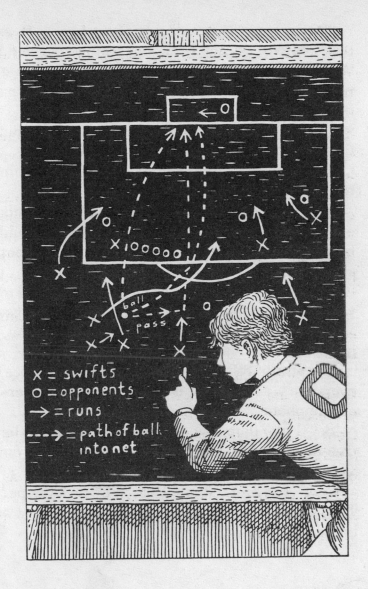

They were still working on the set-piece free-kicks, making decoy runs and seeing who could best bend a banana shot round a wall of bodies when Luke noticed Uncle Ray come racing towards them.

'About time he got here,' Luke muttered. 'Had to pump all the footballs up myself tonight.'

'Hold it, lads,' Ray shouted as he got within range. 'I've got some news for you.'

'Wonder if the new kit has arrived?' Titch said.

'No need to bother about that,' Sanjay told him. 'You won't have one. They don't do kit that small!'

Ray came to a panting halt and they all had to wait a few moments while he got his breath back.

'You ought to join in Luke's fitness training,' his brother laughed.

'Never mind that,' Ray replied. 'Sorry I'm late, everyone. Just had the manager of the Panthers on the phone.'

'So?' Luke demanded, keen to get back to the free-kicks. 'Are they offering to swap Jon for Tubs here or something?'

Tubs shot him a dirty look. 'Why pick on me? They could swap all of us for Jon and still get a bad deal.'

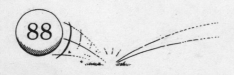

'Just shut up, will you, and listen,' Ray said. 'He rang to tell Jon about the cup draw and he thought we might be interested as well.'

'Why should we want to know who they've got in the cup?' asked Luke.

'Because, dear nephew, it's you! You've drawn Padley Panthers at home in the first round of the Sunday League Cup!'

It took a few seconds for the news to filter through into their numbed brains and then the celebrations began. Gradually, however, the reality of the situation dawned on them and they became very quiet.

'The Panthers are three divisions higher than us,' Big Ben pointed out. 'They'll murder us!'

'No, they won't,' Luke insisted. 'Think positive. The comp's just beaten their High School one–nil. They couldn't even score past Sanjay.'

'Do us a favour, Skipper,' the goalkeeper protested, only half in jest. 'That was my first ever clean sheet. Don't go knocking it.'

'But we had three Panthers on our side then,' Gary reminded them.

'And they're unbeaten in their league,' added Gregg.

'OK, OK, so it won't be easy,' Luke admitted.

'I never said it would be. But they'll probably be thinking we're a walkover . . .'

'They'll be right, too,' Tubs interrupted.

'No they won't,' said Luke, his face aglow with excitement at the prospect of the cup clash. 'We're going to have one or two surprises up our sleeves.'

'Like what?' asked Dad.

'No good trying to pull that double stunt on them,' Gary said. 'Adam will easily spot the difference between me and our kid.'

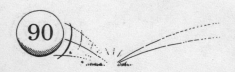

'I've got other ideas, don't worry. This could be the turning point of our season. Imagine . . . we'll be able to run out in our new kit, all flash, like, and then show them how football should really be played.'

'Come off it, Skipper, that's fantasy football stuff,' said Mark, trying to bring Luke back down to earth. 'They're miles better than us.'

'Individually, perhaps,' Luke conceded. 'But football's a team game, men. Good teamwork – that's what it takes to be cup giant-killers!'

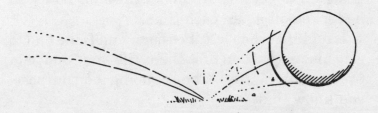

7 Team Tactics

Over the next two weeks at school, Luke and the other Swifts came in for merciless taunting about the cup match.

'We're all going to bring calculators,' the Panthers' top scorer, Matthew, promised. 'This could be a new world record score to put into your little black book, Loony Luke.'

'For us or for you?' Luke queried, straight-faced.

Matthew scoffed at his response. 'What I'm really looking forward to is reading the report of the match in the *Chronicle*. I want to see how their weird sports correspondent will make a fifty–nil massacre sound like a moral victory!'

'One thing's for sure,' Adam added. 'The Sloths' player-manager, chief coach and skipper is bound to get a mention of praise for how well he kicked off again each time!'

Laughing, they left the room, and Luke had to grit his teeth. 'Don't let them rile you,' Jon said from a table nearby. 'They're doing it on purpose, you know that.'

'Well, I'm glad you're not joining in.'

'No need. Everybody knows you're going to be slaughtered,' his cousin replied with a grin. 'Vikesh, our captain, is even thinking of putting a few reserves in the team just to make it a bit less one-sided.'

Luke was furious. 'He'd better not, you tell him that from me. I want to beat the Panthers at full strength so they don't have any excuses.'

Sanjay buried his head in his hands. 'You idiot!' he exclaimed as his face reappeared. 'You've just gone and blown our only chance of escaping a bit more lightly. Looks like I'm gonna have to fetch some wood and nails.'

Luke was puzzled. 'Wood and nails? What for?'

'To board up our goals. That's the only way we'll stop 'em scoring!'

'Rubbish! Remember our secret training,' Luke said with a wink.

'You mean all that nonsense last night on the recky was actually meant to be serious?'

'You bet! I can't wait to see their faces when we do it for real. This is going to be the match of the century.'

'Yeah,' sighed Sanjay. 'A hundred goals at least!'

Despite Sanjay's pessimism, Luke would not be put off. He remained hopeful that his planned tactics might yet upset the favourites. He'd spent hours devising detailed charts and diagrams on his computer, and at the start of yesterday's practice, he'd given a pile of print-outs to each of the Swifts for them to study. He wanted to make sure every player knew their jobs at set-pieces like goalkicks, corners, free-kicks and throw-ins.

'On the video I've spotted some weaknesses in

their defence that we can work on,' he said with pride. 'The Panthers won't know what's hit them.'

'They won't, if we throw all this paper at them,' said Tubs.

'I can't even lift my pile!' joked Titch.

Luke glared at them. 'It's not for throwing, it's for memorizing.'

Brain scratched his head, leafing through all the sheets. 'I can't even read this stuff, Skipper, never mind memorize it.'

'You'll be OK, once we've practised everything,' Luke reassured him. 'When you actually do it, you'll understand. Their fullbacks don't mark very tight. I want you and Dazza to keep switching wings to confuse them and get loads of crosses into the middle for me and Gregg.'

'It'll confuse me too. Can't I stay in one position?' Brain pleaded. 'I know where I'm supposed to be then.'

'So does your marker. If you cut inside and keep moving around, he won't know where to go.'

'Nor will I,' Brain mumbled in reply.

Luke, however, had passed on, developing his theme. 'I want our own fullbacks to overlap down the wings as well, to put extra pressure on their

defenders. You'll find examples of what I mean on page five.'

'Fine by me,' Gary grinned. 'I love to join in the attacks.'

'You can run, I can't,' Tubs complained. 'What about me, Skipper? I'm normally right-back.'

'Yeah, right back off the pitch,' laughed Sanjay.

'This time he's left-back,' Titch said quickly. 'Left back in the changing cabin!'

'Don't listen to them, Tubs,' Luke said. 'You're still in the team. In fact, I've got very special plans for you. Take a good look at page eight and you'll see . . .'

'Right, men, all ready?'

'Ready, Skipper!' they chorused, eager for action.

Before they left the cabin, Luke gazed round at his players, glistening clean and bright in their new all-gold strip with its green numbers. 'Now we look like a real team at last. Let's get out there and get at 'em!'

The skipper led them proudly out of the door and down the steps on to the wet grass, the magazine's title emblazoned across their shirt fronts in large green letters: **GREAT GAME!**

98

The Swifts had chosen this cup clash against the Panthers as the most fitting occasion to wear the prize kit for the first time. They all felt a little strange in it, looking so smart, but only Tubs and Titch had any complaints. The shirts had come in one standard size. They buried Titch, but Tubs was bulging out of his so much he couldn't even tuck it into his tight shorts.

The Panthers, cool and menacing in their deep-blue strip with its red trim, were already out on the pitch. 'Aarrghh!' screamed Matthew, falling backwards in exaggerated fashion as the golden Swifts ran by. 'My eyes! I'm blinded. Why didn't somebody warn me?'

Adam, too, shielded his eyes. 'Hey, lads, the Sloths are trying to dazzle us!'

'Let them have their stupid jokes,' Luke called out. 'It won't be our kit that dazzles them today, it'll be our football.'

Vikesh, the Panthers' captain, wore a pair of borrowed shades for the toss-up. 'Heard all about you, Loony Luke, the soccer mastermind,' he smirked. 'Who won the F.A. Cup in 1946 then?'

'Derby County,' Luke replied instantly. 'They beat Charlton Athletic four–one after extra time. Next question.'

'Heads or tails?' Vikesh grunted, spinning a coin.

'Tails!'

'Huh! That's the only thing you'll win today,' Vikesh warned.

'We'll have kick-off,' Luke announced, instead of choosing ends. With little or no wind, there was no particular advantage to be gained that way. He had another plan in mind.

As rehearsed, Luke and Gregg started the ball rolling and the skipper immediately tapped it back to where Tubs was lurking behind them in the centre-circle. He gave the ball a mighty punt, hoping to catch Ravi off guard in the Panthers' goal. He did. Ravi was still taking a swig from a water bottle he kept behind a post and only a warning shout from Adam as the ball sailed over everyone's heads alerted the keeper to the danger.

Ravi dropped the bottle and scrambled desperately over to his far post, but it was too late. The ball beat him, and, as he lost his footing and his dignity, it bounced agonizingly just wide of the upright for a goalkick. There were hoots of derision from his teammates as he picked himself up, glaring at his spilt water and the mud all down one side of his kit. There had been heavy overnight rain, and both goalmouths of the Swillsby pitch were spattered with small puddles. He was not amused.

'Great effort, Tubs!' Luke cried. 'That's shown 'em we mean business!'

'Right, you've asked for it now, Sloths!' Vikesh called out.

'Oh, no!' groaned Sanjay to himself. 'I told Luke we shouldn't upset them. I still think we're going to need that plywood.'

Sanjay soon got his own outfit dirty, too, flinging himself down at the feet of an opponent to smother the ball. But his distribution was careless. Brain wasn't expecting a quick, thrown pass and he was easily robbed. Matthew found himself in possession outside the area and thumped the ball high towards goal, knowing that Sanjay was hopelessly out of position. His

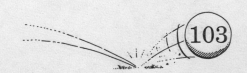

cry of 'Goal!' died in his throat as the ball clunked off the crossbar and rebounded straight back into Sanjay's grateful arms.

'Perhaps it's going to be my lucky day,' the keeper breathed in relief.

Sanjay had reason to think otherwise just a minute later when Jon made his mark on the game. Sidestepping past Gary's tackle, he accelerated smoothly through two more lunges and fancied a pop at goal as Big Ben moved across to bar his path. He struck the ball powerfully with his left instep and watched it snake towards the far post. Jon had a clearer view than the keeper who'd been partially unsighted at first by his tall defender. As he dived full-length, Sanjay thought he had the shot covered until the ball dipped cruelly at the last split-second and evaded his grasp.

'One–nil!' shouted Matthew. 'The first of many. Get the calculators out, lads, we're going to run riot here.'

'Good goal, Johan,' Luke congratulated his cousin as he trotted back for the re-start. 'Have to give you that one. Real class.'

'Watch out for another bomber, Ravi!' Vikesh cried out as Tubs geared himself up for a possible repeat performance. Luke, though, decided

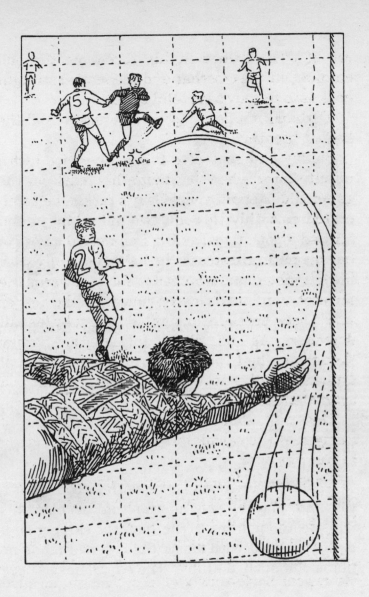

on one of their other prepared set-pieces. They'd had so much practice at kicking-off in their games that they had plenty of moves to choose from. He swept the ball out to Dazza, darting inside from the right touchline, and the winger hared for goal. He was too quick for Adam, who mistimed his challenge, stretching out his leg and catching Dazza on the heel.

'*Penalty!*' screamed Luke, both as commentator and player, and as the referee blew his whistle and pointed to the spot, the skipper suddenly realized with shock that he had made no plans for such a thing. They had never been

given a penalty – for the simple reason that the Swifts rarely got as far as their opponents' penalty area.

His players looked towards him in confusion. 'I'll take it!' Luke announced firmly. 'Skipper's responsibility.'

Luke was baited non-stop as he settled the ball on the muddy penalty spot and then stood up, taking several deep breaths to try and control his pounding heart.

'This should be funny,' came a voice that sounded very much like Matthew's. 'This could go anywhere . . .'

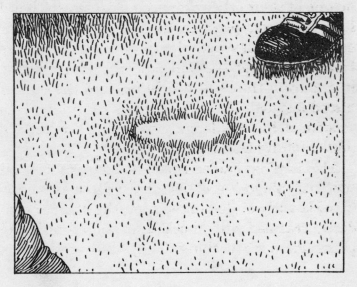

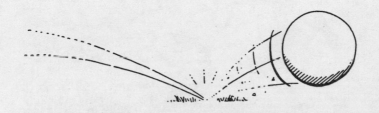

8 Fantasy Football

Ravi stood tall on the goal-line, wanting to impose the full force of his commanding personality on the kicker. Luke, on the other hand, was simply trying to convince himself that nobody was unbeatable.

He had never had the chance to take a penalty before in a proper game and was so nervous that even his commentary had dried up. The goal seemed to shrink in size to that of the one in his back garden and Ravi looked massive, his bulky figure expanding to fill the space.

As the whistle blew, Luke moved in on legs that didn't feel as though they belonged to him, like wading through custard. He had no idea which side of the goal to put the ball. But that hardly mattered. He doubted whether it would go where he aimed, anyway.

The final result was catastrophic. As he reached the ball, his standing foot slipped from underneath him in the mud. He toppled backwards and sent the ball trickling pathetically towards Ravi who only had to bend down and pick it up to make the save.

Hilarious laughter swirled around him and

Luke lay flat on his back, wishing the mud would suck him down out of sight. It was the most embarrassing moment in his whole life.

'Come in, number nine, your time's up!' came a cackle from the large group of Panthers' supporters.

'Never mind, Skipper, get up,' said Brain, offering a helping hand. 'At least you got it on target!'

The break in play for the penalty and all the joking that followed seemed to distract the Panthers from the real job in hand. Already ahead and with further goals apparently there for the taking whenever they wished, their mood became casual, almost lazy, and their football sloppy. Each of the players dwelt too long on the ball, wanting to show off their skills and fancy footwork, instead of passing it on to a teammate to continue the move. Attacks lost momentum and broke down as the ball was given away or the dribbler tried to beat one man too many and was crowded out.

The Panthers' defence, too, grew careless and they had only themselves to blame when slack marking enabled the Swifts to equalize just before half-time. Dazza was allowed to run free

down the wing and had time to steady himself and look up before his centre found Gregg in oceans of space inside the penalty area. The younger twin made the most of his good fortune. His first touch wasn't brilliant, but as the ball began to bobble away from him, Gregg was still able to drag it back under control, turn and lash his shot past the helpless Ravi.

'*One goal apiece at the interval,*' yapped Luke's commentary a minute later, '*and the Swifts are producing their best performance of the season. Have the Panthers underestimated their opponents? Will the underdogs have their day? Join us again in the second half to find out . . .*'

Nobody mentioned Luke's penalty miss during the breather. It was almost forgotten in the Swifts' bewilderment at finding themselves on level terms.

'Hey! We could even win this match yet,' Gary cried. 'They're playing rubbish.'

'I told you so,' Luke stressed. 'But it's our good teamwork that's doing it. We're not letting them play. They didn't expect a tough battle like this and now they can't get their act together properly.'

'Look at them over there,' Titch said, pointing to the agitated group some distance away. 'They're arguing among themselves. Jon's having to separate Adam and Ravi!'

'We've got 'em rattled!' Luke exclaimed. 'This is it, men. If we can get another quick goal, they'll crack completely.'

Sanjay wasn't so sure. 'They look in a mean mood,' he muttered as the teams lined up again. 'Prepare to repel boarders, defence!'

The Panthers hit them with everything they had at the start of the second half, fired up after the heated arguments and the half-time roasting from their angry manager. Their attacks were direct and fierce but lacked control and cool finishing. Time after time the ball was pumped high into the Swifts' penalty area rather than being passed man-to-man along the ground as the Panthers normally liked to play their football.

Sanjay felt that they were testing him out, expecting him to drop his usual clangers. But he was kept so busy under the constant bombardment that it had the opposite effect. The unpredictable keeper was played into top form and he clutched almost every cross out of the air

113

cleanly and safely. Nor did he have to rely too much on 'Lady Luck' smiling down upon him. From one of the many corners, Sanjay pulled off a spectacular double save, firstly blocking Matthew's close-range header and then holding on to Jon's flick that seemed destined for the top corner of the goal.

The Panthers were becoming more and more frustrated at their own failure to score again. Vikesh was the worst culprit, berating his players every time they made a mistake, causing some to answer him back. What little remained of their team spirit entirely disintegrated.

They began to argue, too, with the referee's decisions and commit niggling fouls. When Vikesh tripped Brain from behind as he tried to dribble his way towards goal, it earned the Panthers' captain a stern lecture from the referee and the Swifts a direct free-kick just outside the 'D' of the penalty area. As the Panthers half-heartedly formed a human wall, Luke directed the winger to take it himself. 'Either foot, Brain, whichever takes your fancy!'

Several of the Swifts made their well-practised decoy runs to try and fool defenders. Then Luke sprinted forwards, looking as if he

was going to hit it, but ran over the top of the ball at the last moment as Brain followed up. A couple of players broke away from the wall, thinking the ball was going to be knocked across to Tubs who was prowling about nearby. Instead, Brain's accurate, right-footed strike pierced the gap where they'd been standing. Ravi was unsighted and could make only a belated, token dive, flapping at the ball as it flew past him high into the net.

'It worked, it worked!' Luke yelled, forgetting all about his usual commentary in the heat of the moment. 'What a bullet free-kick!'

'This is a nightmare!' Matthew moaned. 'C'mon, get a grip, everybody. We can't let this lot beat us!'

It was too late to rally the troops. Vikesh seemed to have lost interest and too many of the players were bickering, blaming each other for the mess that they were in.

'I've never seen Jon's team like this,' Ray said to his brother. 'They're not used to being behind. They don't know how to react.'

Philip lowered the camera briefly and grinned. 'They're demoralized. There's no way they'll be able to fight back. The Panthers will

have to call themselves the "Pussycats" from now on!'

The men were right. Too many heads of the visitors had gone down and the Swifts dictated the remainder of the match. Still working hard for each other, they won every fifty-fifty ball in midfield, snuffing out any Panthers' attacks early and then mounting some dangerous raids of their own to earn a spate of corners. Brain floated these teasingly into the goalmouth from either side and only Ravi's acrobatic saves were preventing further goals.

Another one, however, simply had to come. And when it did, it came from a most unlikely source. Dazza won a throw-in on the right and was about to take it himself when he remembercd the instructions on page eight of Luke's printed dossier. He left it to Tubs. Lumbering up to the touchline, Tubs used all the muscle strength in his powerful arms to hurl the ball across into the heart of the Panthers' territory where Gregg rose to backhead it further on.

Its unexpected arrival caused chaos in the six-yard box and finally the ball was squirted out of the ruck of heaving bodies towards an unmarked attacker. It was the skipper! Luke had time to

balance himself and, as he drew his foot back to shoot, images of Jon in the garden flashed into his mind and the hushed commentary echoed his cousin's advice, *'Don't panic, stay cool, keep it low.'*

Luke concentrated all his attention on keeping his knee and body over the ball so as not to balloon it skywards, and as a tackler lunged in, he let fly. Ravi got down well to the skimming shot, but the ball squirmed under his diving body and was deflected through the legs of a defender on the line to ripple the netting.

'Yeeesss!' Luke raised his arms to the heavens, fists clenched and eyes tight shut, soaking in the elation of scoring their third goal. It was a better feeling than logging all the soccer statistics in the world into his little black notebook!

The delirious skipper was carried back to the halfway line by his teammates, helped by an almost unrecognizable mudheap whose huge white grin was the only telltale factor. 'You're a hero, Skipper!' Sanjay yelled. 'You've won us the match!'

Luke was so stunned by the miracle that had taken place, he had no recollection afterwards of the last few minutes of the cup-tie. He had run

himself silly, trying to be everywhere on the pitch at the same time, and had now ground to a complete standstill. Even his commentary was on automatic pilot. He only knew it was all over when his cousin came to shake his hand.

'One for the record books, that,' Jon smiled, sporting in defeat. 'The Swifts' first ever victory. Well done.'

'Yeah!' Luke gasped, jabbing at the printed words on the front of his mud-stained, gold shirt. 'Great Game! That's exactly what football is. You can never tell what's going to happen.'

'Three—one! Frosty sure won't believe it when he hears this result,' Sanjay butted in, shaking his own head at the wonder of it. 'He'll think we've all gone mad!'

'He already knows *I* have,' Luke laughed. 'Soccer mad!'

THE END

ABOUT THE AUTHOR

ROB CHILDS is a Leicestershire teacher with many years experience of coaching and organizing school and area representative sports teams. He now divides his week between teaching and writing and is the author of a number of previous titles for the Transworld lists, most notably *The Big Match* and other titles about Chris and Andrew Weston, two football-mad brothers. There are nine titles in this series currently in print.

Soccer Mad is the first title in a new series of footballing titles about Luke and his friends; a second title, *All Goalies are Crazy*, follows in Corgi Yearling Books later this year.

Don't miss the second title in the action-packed *Soccer Mad* series, coming soon from Corgi Yearling Books!

ALL GOALIES ARE CRAZY

ROB CHILDS

No-one enjoys keeping goal so much as Sanjay Mistry – the regular, if unpredictable, goalie both for the school team and for the Swillsby Swifts, the Sunday league team led by soccer-mad Luke Crawford. But after Sanjay makes a series of terrible match-losing blunders, Luke decides that it's time someone else had a go at playing in goal – himself!

Determined to prove himself as the number one goalie, Sanjay rises to the challenge with some outstanding and acrobatic saves. But Luke's enthusiasm and crazy antics make him a surprisingly serious rival . . .

0 440 863503

SOCCER AT SANDFORD

ROB CHILDS

'We're going to have a fantastic season!'

Jeff Thompson is delighted to be picked as captain of Sandford School's football team. With an enthusiastic new teacher and a team full of talent – not least that of loner Gary Clarke, with his flashes of goal-scoring brilliance – he is determined to lead Sandford to success. Their goal is the important League Championship – and their main rivals are Tanby, who they must first meet in a vital Cup-tie . . .

From kick-off to the final whistle, through success and disappointment, penalties and corners, to the final nail-biting matches of the season, follow the action and the excitement as the young footballers of Sandford School learn how to develop their skills and mould together as a real team – a team who are determined to win by playing the best football possible!

0 440 86318X

THE BIG PRIZE

ROB CHILDS

*'Huh! Some lucky mascot you're gonna be –
Selworth have got no chance this afternoon with
you around!'*

Everything seems to be going great for Chris
Weston. First he wins the prize of being chosen
to be the mascot for the local football league club
for their next F.A. Cup match. Then he is picked
to play in goal for his school team on the
morning of the same day.

But then disaster strikes and Chris can hardly
walk, let alone run out on to a pitch. Has his luck
suddenly changed for the worse? And will he
miss his chance of being a mascot?

A lively and action-packed new title in a popular
series about two football-mad brothers.

0 552 528234

THE BIG GAME

ROB CHILDS

Football! A great game – best in the world!

It's September, and Andrew Weston can hardly wait to get back to school. For this year he is to play in the school football team, and Andrew is sure that his skills in defence will help Danebridge win every match.

But Andrew and his younger brother Chris – a promising goalkeeper – are in action even sooner when they take part in an annual six-a-side football tournament. When a young winger for the Selworth team gives Andrew a few bad moments, Andrew suspects that his debut match for the school team won't be easy at all. For their first opponents are to be . . . Selworth!

0 552 528048